BOO-HOO MOO

By Margie Palatini
Illustrated by Keith Graves

KATHERINE TEGEN BOOKS
An Imprint of HarperCollins*Publishers*

Boo-Hoo Moo
Text copyright © 2009 by Margie Palatini Illustrations copyright © 2009 by Keith Graves
Manufactured in China.
All rights reserved. No part of this book may be used or reproduced in any manner whatsoever without written permission except in the case of brief quotations embodied in critical articles and reviews. For information address HarperCollins Children's Books, a division of HarperCollins Publishers, 1350 Avenue of the Americas, New York, NY 10019.
www.harpercollinschildrens.com

Library of Congress Cataloging-in-Publication Data
Palatini, Margie.
Boo-hoo moo / by Margie Palatini ; illustrated by Keith Graves. — 1st ed.
p. cm.
Summary: When Hilda Mae Heifer's trademark "moo" starts sounding even worse, the other animals decide she is lonely and hold auditions to find her some singing partners.
ISBN 978-0-06-114375-5 (trade bdg.) — ISBN 978-0-06-114376-2 (lib. bdg.)
[1. Cows—Fiction. 2. Domestic animals—Fiction. 3. Animal sounds—Fiction. 4. Humorous stories.] I. Graves, Keith, ill. II. Title.
PZ7.P1755Bl 2008 2007024417
[E]—dc22 CIP
AC

Typography by Jeanne L. Hogle

1 2 3 4 5 6 7 8 9 10

❖

First Edition

For Jamie, our favorite "solo act"—who is always on key.
—M.P.
To gloomy cows everywhere. Chin up, girls.
—K.G.
Next!

“Mi-mi-Mo

Hilda Mae Heifer was down in the dumps.
Feeling low. Sounding like it too.
Even her moo was blue.

oo-OOOOO.
BOO-HOO-MOO..."

The goose shook his head.
"Wow. That is one unhappy cow."

"BOO-HOO-MOOOO."

"She sounds miserable," said the hen.
"I second that," said the pig. "That blubbering bovine is ruining my siestas. I haven't slept in days!"

Even when Hilda was at her happiest, she was far from the best singer. Now these new blue boo-hoo moos were more than everyone's ears and earplugs could take.

But what could they do?

Not much.
Day . . . after day . . . after day . . .

Hilda hung her head and blue mooed from barn to pasture. Pasture to barn.

And finally, she would just come home and stall out.

"I believe Hilda is lonely," said the cat. "I don't think she likes singing solo."

"Mi-mi-MOOOOOOOO-Boo-HOO-mooooo!"

The pig covered his ears. "I'm not fond of her singing solo myself."

"She needs help," said the cat.

"I couldn't agree more!" said the pig.

"What *Hilda* needs is a partner," continued the cat. "I bet a duet would be just the thing to lift her spirits!"

The hen gathered her chickies and clucked. "Why, of course. Two is always better than one! *Especially* if the other can carry a tune."

"Then—why not a trio?" added the goose.

"A quartet!" chimed in the pig. "The more the merrier! I know it will make me happy."

So the four decided to help Hilda Mae lose her Boo-Hoo Blues. They would find the off-key cow some singing partners.

But just who to moo? That was a difficult decision.

They made a list:

1. Singers who didn't sing too loudly. ✓
2. Singers who didn't sing too softly. ✓
3. Singers who had talent! ✓ ✓ ✓

"Actually," said the cat, "I think a **Mew mew mew** would sound lovely with a **Moo moo moo**. In fact, I spent a good deal of my youth warbling at the moon. I believe I will sing with Hilda."

"YOU?" cried the surprised threesome.

The goose waddled over to the cat and cleared his throat.

"Uh, just a minute there, fuzz face. If any of us is going to have a sing-along with the cow . . . it's yours truly."

"YOU?"

"My honking is legendary. Get a load of this—

"Honk honk
honk
honk honk
h-h-h-honk!"
"Mi mi
mew mew
mew.
mew."

The hen bristled. "*Ha!* My cluck is *positively* operatic!

"Cluck cluck cluck cluck. Cluck cluck. P'awk! P'awk! P'awk!"

The pig interrupted the squawking soprano. "It is not crowing but crooning that is needed here. I am the proper baritone to complement that cow."

"YOU?"

"Me," said the pig. "Listen and observe: **Oink oink oink oink!"**

"Ha! **P'awk cluck cluck cluck!"**

"Oink oink oink—snort!"

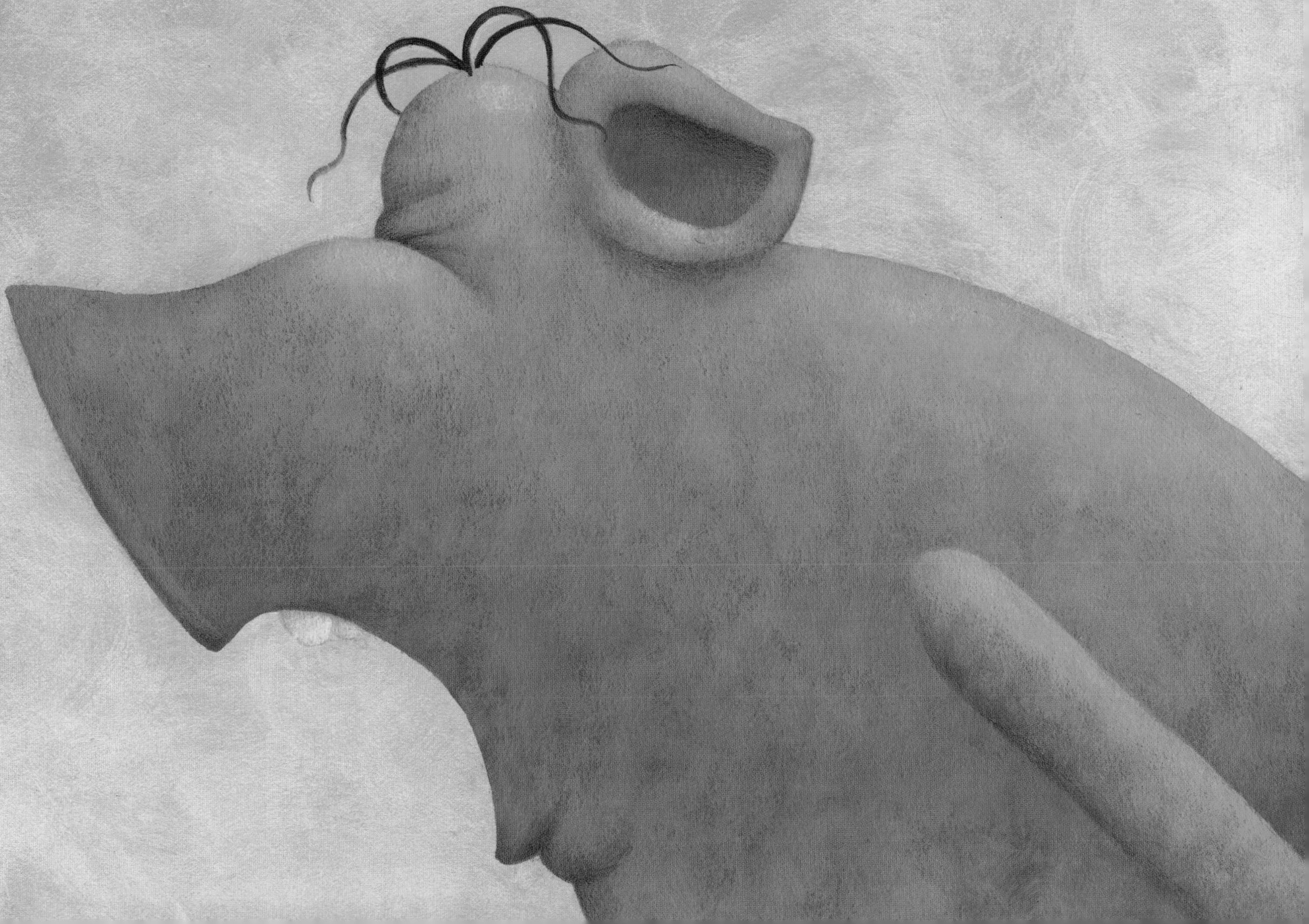

"Hold it down! Zip it! Quiet!" shouted the goose.

The four stared at one another. Then the goose giggled.

"You know something . . . that wasn't half bad. In fact, it sounded pretty good! Let's try that again." He tapped his foot on a downbeat. "And a one—and a two—"

“Honk honk honk cluck cluck
snort me-ooooooOOW!”

The pig blushed with excitement. "Oh, my dears, we should form a chorus and sing along with Hilda!"

"But we need more singers for a whole chorus," advised the cat.

Many more singers, they all agreed.

Auditions began that very afternoon. There was quite a turnout. . . .

"Baaa-baaa-b-a-a-

It was quite a chorus. The four were certain no one would be able to hear a wayward mi-mi-moo from Hilda even if they tried.

They all applauded.

"Fabulous! Superb! We love it!"

The question was . . . would Miss Heifer? And would she tra-la-la along with them?

The sun was setting just as Hilda bounded across the meadow. The barnyard chorus was so excited they burst into song to greet her.

"Mew!"

"Baa-aaa-aaaa-aaaa!"

"Honk!"

"Nay!"

Hilda was baffled. Bewildered. Completely befuddled.

"HuuuUUH?"

"You ain't heard nothin' yet!" honked the goose.

"Doodle-doodle-doo."

"Bow-wow-oh-wow!"

"Ribbit!"

"Squeak!"

"Oink!"

"Squawk! P'awk!"

"Moo-moo-moo."

"Surprise!" sang out the cat.
"We formed a chorus so you could sing
along with friends. Now you won't be sad or
lonely, and your moo will never be blue again!"

Hilda grinned. "Me? Mi-Mi-MOO with all of yooooooooou? How too-toooo grand. But . . . I've given up singing."

"What?"

"To be honest," said Hilda, "I don't think I can really sing."

The pig raised his eyebrows. "*No kidding.*"

Hilda nodded. "Yup. I'm giving it up."

The pig immediately removed his earplugs and smiled broadly. "Bravo! A gloriously intelligent decision, my dear!"

The cow grinned. "It's true. I am definitely not a singer. I have the soul of a *dancer*! I'm a heifer who's a hoofer! Who knew I was so light on my feet!"

Thump

Thump

Thumpa-thumpa

Boom